Helping Hospital

A Community Helpers Book

For Clelia—
Thank you for your wonderfully
creative idea that you let me run wild with.

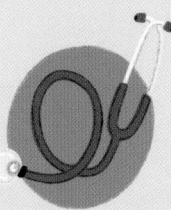

And for all the amazing people working
in hospitals who take care of all of us.
Thank you for all that you do!
—L.W.

The artist used her iPad Pro and consumed copious amounts of coffee while
listening to many, many, many audio books to create the digital illustrations for this book.
Typography by Erica De Chavez 21 22 23 24 25 RTLO 10 9 8 7 6 5 4 3 2 1 ❖ First Edition

Helping Hospital

A Community Helpers Book

Lindsay Ward

HARPER

An Imprint of HarperCollinsPublishers

WELCOME TO HELPING HOSPITAL!

These are all the people who work here:

DOCTORS

NURSES

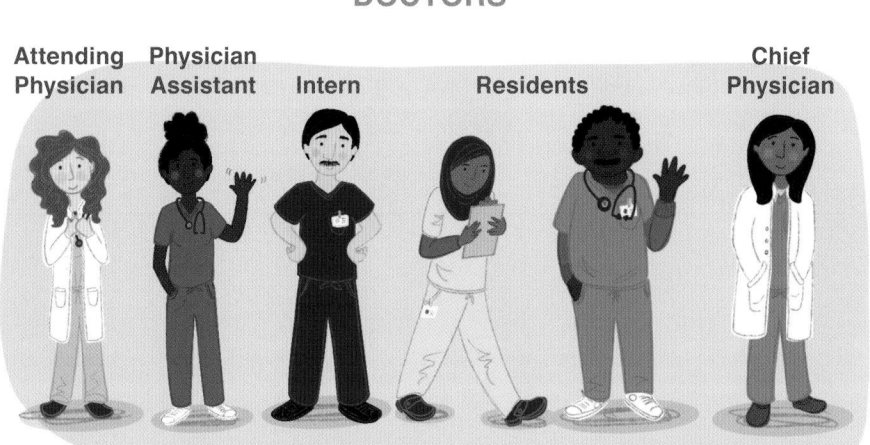

ADVANCED PRACTITIONERS

LABORATORY

PHARMACY

Wow. That's a lot of people! Can you count them all?

Each job is important.

REHABILITATION

Physical Therapist

Speech Therapist

Respiratory Therapist

FIRST RESPONDERS

EMT

Paramedic

Medevac Pilot

PASTORAL SERVICES

Hospital Chaplain

MEDICAL TECHNOLOGISTS

MRI

Ultrasound

X-Ray

CAT Scan

OPERATING ROOM

Surgical Tech

Anesthesiologist

Surgeons

FOOD SERVICES

Nutritionist

Cook

Dishwasher

Food Service Assistant

ENVIRONMENTAL SERVICES

Housekeepers

Volunteers

Transportation Assistant

CAUTION WET FLOOR

Everyone at Helping Hospital works together
to keep the town of Honey Hill safe and healthy.

Lots of people are visiting Helping Hospital today.

HOSPITAL HOUSEKEEPER
This is Cal. She is in charge of changing, moving, and cleaning all the laundry in the hospital. Wow! That's a lot of sheets!

HOSPITAL HOUSEKEEPER
This is Mr. Fixit. He has one of the most important jobs in the hospital. Mr. Fixit keeps everything clean and helps prevent people from picking up germs while visiting Helping Hospital.

CAUTION
WET FLOOR

This is Emmy. Her mommy is going to have a baby! Soon Emmy will have a new brother or sister.

PATIENT REPRESENTATIVE
This is May. She educates, ensures the safety of, and provides a voice for patients at Helping Hospital.

MEDEVAC PILOT
This is Eloise. She's a **medevac helicopter** pilot. She flies patients to Helping Hospital in an emergency.

RECEPTION

Hello. Welcome to Helping Hospital. How may I help you today?

Oh no! Leo hurt his arm. An orderly helps Leo get into a **wheelchair**. The transportation assistant, Leo, and his dad wait to ride the elevator.

WELCOME

ADMISSIONS CLERK
This is Gabe. He's in charge of admitting patients to Helping Hospital.

Annabelle is here for a checkup. Last time she had to get a **shot**. She is a little nervous about visiting the **doctor** today.

Helping Hospital is a big place. There are lots of departments. Each one helps in different ways.

Can you guess which departments Emmy, Leo, and Annabelle will visit today?

Surgery

Pre-Op

Obstetrics/Gynecology

Pediatrics

Nursery

Emergency Room

Emergency Room Lobby

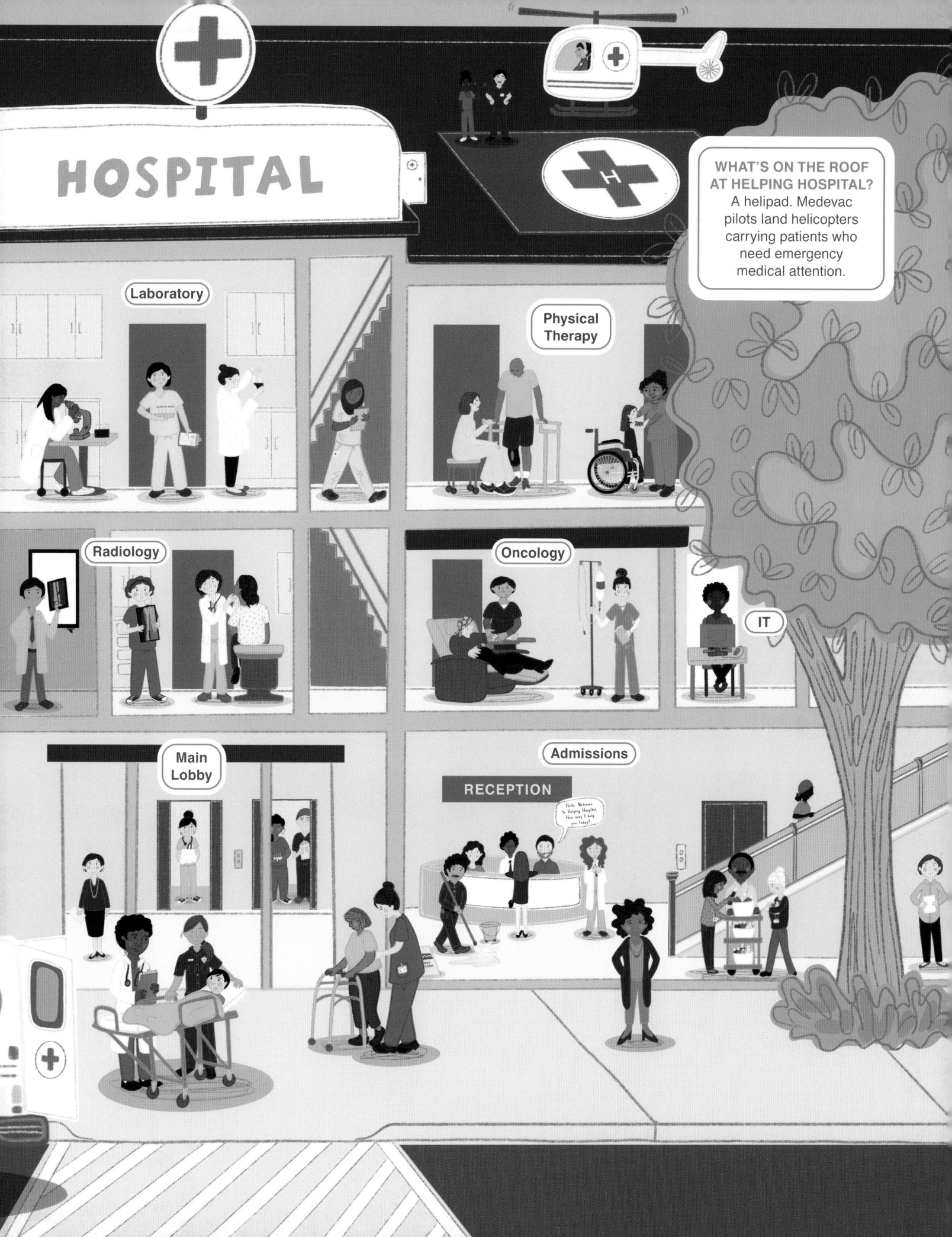

HOSPITAL

Laboratory

Physical Therapy

WHAT'S ON THE ROOF AT HELPING HOSPITAL?
A helipad. Medevac pilots land helicopters carrying patients who need emergency medical attention.

Radiology

Oncology

IT

Main Lobby

Admissions

RECEPTION

Hello. Welcome to Helping Hospital. How may I help you today?

Emmy and her mommy have finished checking in with the admissions clerk in the obstetrics/gynecology department.

Can you find Emmy and her mommy in the waiting room?

The **nurse** calls them.
It's time to see the doctor.

Helping Hospital has a team of nurses who take care of every patient.
Nurses monitor patients closely and communicate information to doctors.

REGISTERED NURSE (RN)

A nurse who has graduated nursing school and has a license to practice nursing.

NURSE PRACTITIONER (NP)

An advanced practice RN who cares for patients.

NURSE MANAGER

Supervises a staff of nurses at a hospital.

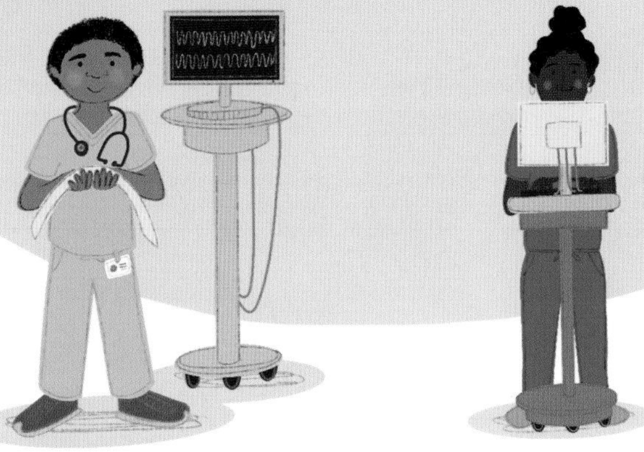

TELEMETRY NURSE
Specializes in cardiology and monitors their patients' heart rhythm.

CLINICAL NURSE SPECIALIST
An advanced practice RN who provides advice on specific conditions and treatments for patients.

ORTHOPEDIC NURSE

Provides care for patients with issues and diseases relating to bones and joints.

CARDIOVASCULAR NURSE

Provides care for patients with heart conditions or diseases.

DIALYSIS NURSE

Provides care for patients with kidney disease.

PSYCHIATRIC-MENTAL HEALTH NURSE PRACTITIONER

An advanced practice RN who provides care to mental health patients.

Nurses work in many different departments of the hospital.
Some nurses take care of patients who need help with specific parts of their body.

Some nurses take care of specific types of patients.

ONCOLOGY NURSE

Provides care for cancer patients.

PEDIATRIC NURSE

Provides care for children.

NEONATAL INTENSIVE CARE UNIT NURSE

Cares for newborn infants.

LABOR & DELIVERY NURSE

Assists and cares for pregnant women throughout labor and delivery.

RADIOLOGY NURSE

Cares for patients preparing for imaging procedures such as X-rays, ultrasounds, CT scans, and MRIs.

Some nurses take care of patients in an emergency or in need of critical care.

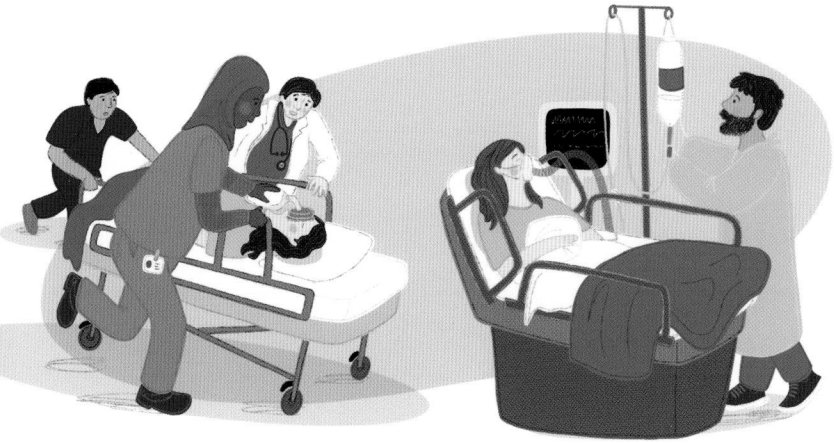

EMERGENCY ROOM NURSE
An RN who cares for patients in an emergency room.

INTENSIVE CARE UNIT NURSE
An RN who cares for critically ill patients in the intensive care unit (ICU).

Some nurses take care of patients who need surgery.

SURGICAL NURSE
Provides care to surgical patients before, during, and after surgery.

POST-ANESTHESIA CARE UNIT NURSE
Monitors overall care of patients after receiving anesthesia for surgery.

They are very important and keep Helping Hospital running smoothly.
Did you know there were so many different types of nurses?

Nurse Ned is going to take a few vitals and note any information the doctor needs to know.

⌇⌇⌇	89 bpm	**Heart Rate**	The number of times your heart beats per minute.
⌇⌇⌇	120/80	**Blood Pressure**	The force of blood pushing against the artery walls.
⌇⌇	99 %	**Oxygen Level**	How much oxygen is in your blood.
⌇	16 rpm	**Respiratory Rate**	The number of breaths you take per minute.
	98.6 °F	**Temperature**	How warm or cool your body is.

Vital signs show doctors, nurses, and other workers how a **patient** is doing.

Nurse Ned takes Emmy's mommy's **blood pressure**.

Emmy waits patiently with her mommy. A few minutes later, there's a knock at the door.

Hello, Annie, it's nice to see you again. Let's see how the baby's doing today.

Doctor Safer is an obstetrician, or OB. An obstetrician takes care of women during pregnancy and helps deliver babies.

There are many different types of doctors who work at Helping Hospital.

DOCTORS WHO SPECIALIZE IN PARTS OF THE BODY

OPHTHALMOLOGIST
Specializes in eye and vision care.

NEUROLOGIST
Specializes in the brain, spine, and nerves.

PSYCHIATRIST
Specializes in mental health.

OTOLARYNGOLOGIST
Specializes in the ears, nose, and throat.

PULMONOLOGIST
Specializes in the lungs and heart.

CARDIOLOGIST
Helps patients with heart conditions and diseases.

RHEUMATOLOGIST
Specializes in joints and autoimmune conditions.

GASTROENTEROLOGIST
Specializes in the digestive tract.

NEPHROLOGIST
Specializes in diseases relating to the kidneys.

PODIATRIST
Specializes in feet, ankles, and lower legs.

UROLOGIST
Specializes in the urinary tract.

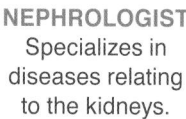

DOCTORS WHO SPECIALIZE IN SYSTEMS IN THE BODY

ENDOCRINOLOGIST
Specializes in hormones, glands, and metabolism.

HEMATOLOGIST
Specializes in the study of blood and blood disorders.

PATHOLOGIST
Studies body fluids and tissues.

DERMATOLOGIST
Specializes in skin disorders and diseases.

ALLERGIST/ IMMUNOLOGIST
Helps patients with immune system disorders.

Some doctors oversee and manage the rest of the doctors in a hospital.

PHYSICIAN EXECUTIVE (NONCLINICAL DOCTOR)
Manages all the doctors at the hospital.

SURGEON
Specializes in different areas of the body to perform surgery on patients.

EMERGENCY MEDICINE
Treats patients in the emergency room.

DOCTORS WHO SPECIALIZE IN THE WHOLE BODY

CRITICAL CARE

ANESTHESIOLOGIST

Treats patients who are critically injured or sick in the intensive care unit.

Administers pain medication to patients during surgery.

INFECTIOUS DISEASE
Treats patients with infectious diseases.

SPORTS MEDICINE

RADIOLOGIST
Specializes in diagnosing and treating patients using imaging technology.

Helps treat patients active in sports.

Some doctors take care of specific types of patients.

PEDIATRICIAN

OBSTETRICIAN/ GYNECOLOGIST

FAMILY

ONCOLOGIST

Treats and helps patients with cancer.

Manages the health of children.

Specializes in women's health care and delivers babies.

Provides health care to patients of all ages.

Have any of these types of doctors ever helped you?

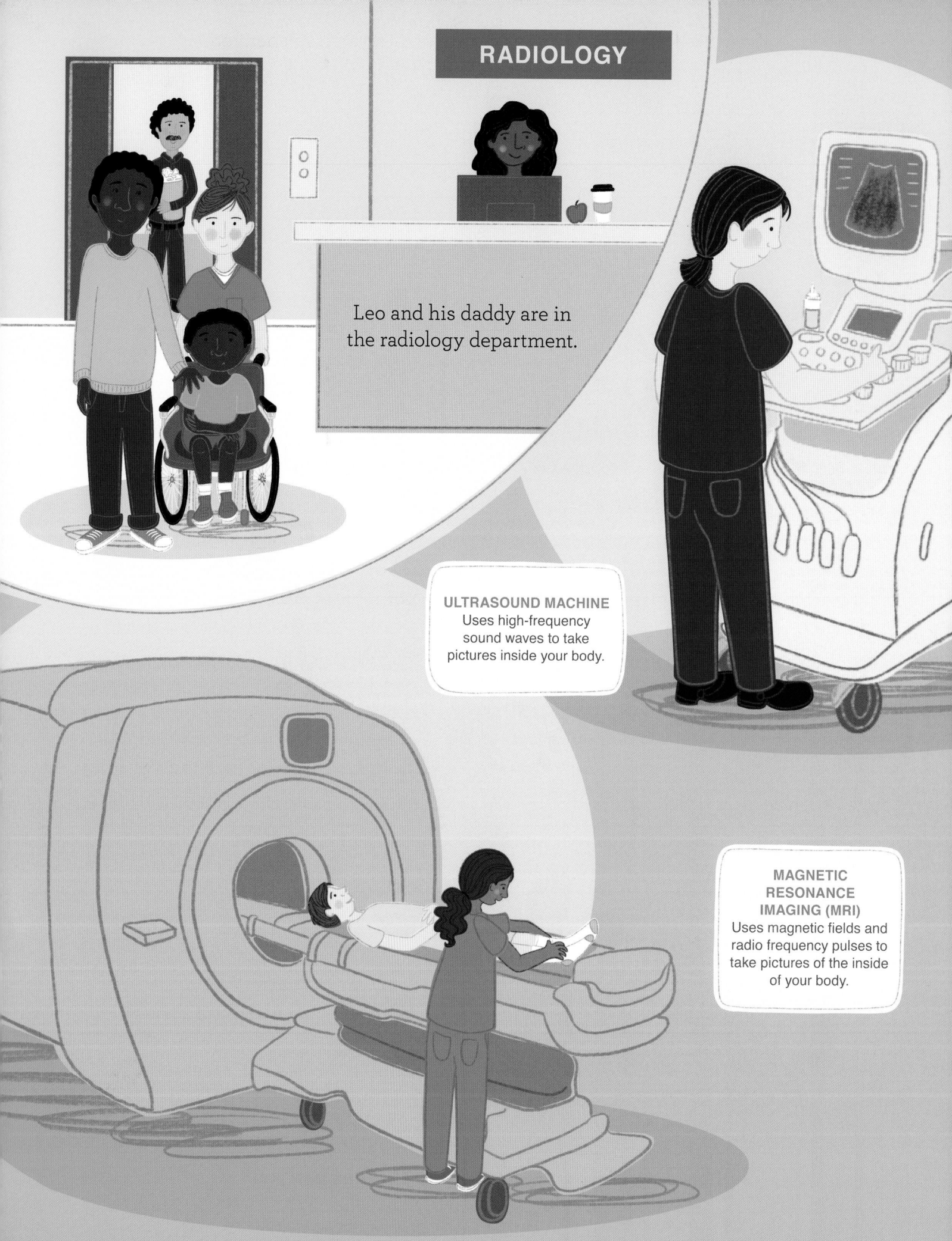

RADIOLOGY

Leo and his daddy are in the radiology department.

ULTRASOUND MACHINE
Uses high-frequency sound waves to take pictures inside your body.

MAGNETIC RESONANCE IMAGING (MRI)
Uses magnetic fields and radio frequency pulses to take pictures of the inside of your body.

There are lots of different machines here. Each one is operated by a technologist and used to help people in different ways.

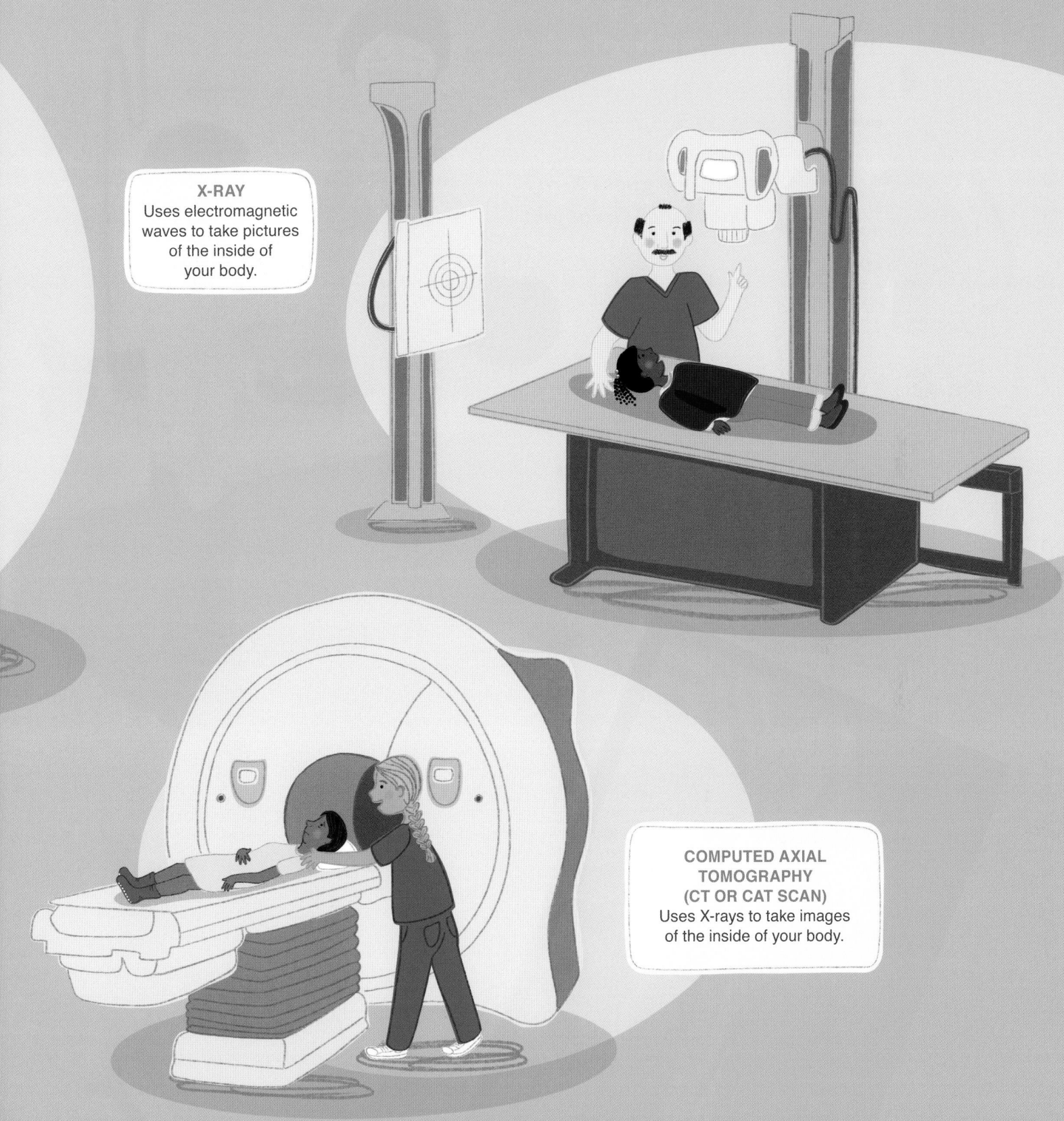

X-RAY
Uses electromagnetic waves to take pictures of the inside of your body.

COMPUTED AXIAL TOMOGRAPHY (CT OR CAT SCAN)
Uses X-rays to take images of the inside of your body.

Which machine do you think will help Leo?

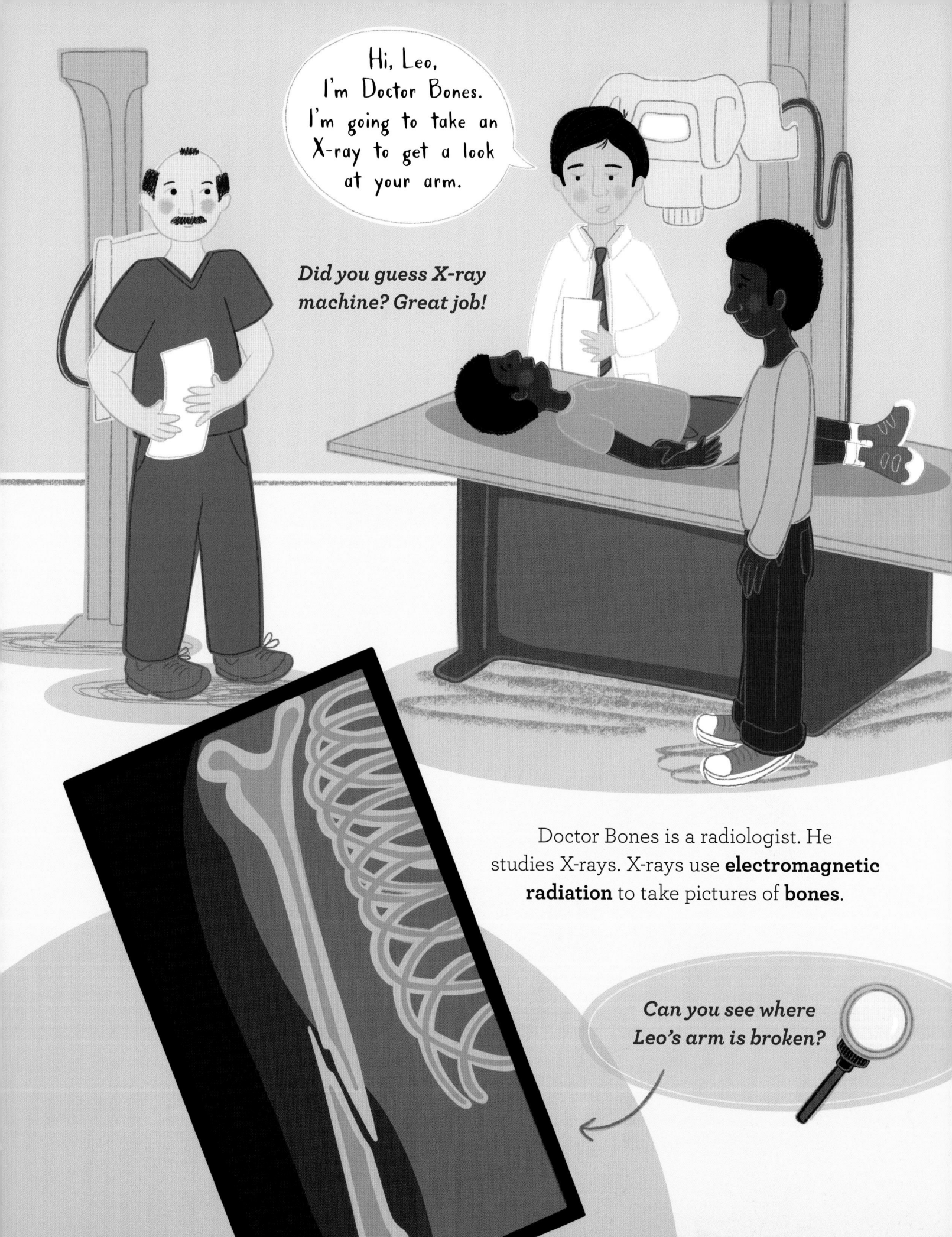

Uh-oh, Leo broke his **humerus**. And there's nothing funny about that!

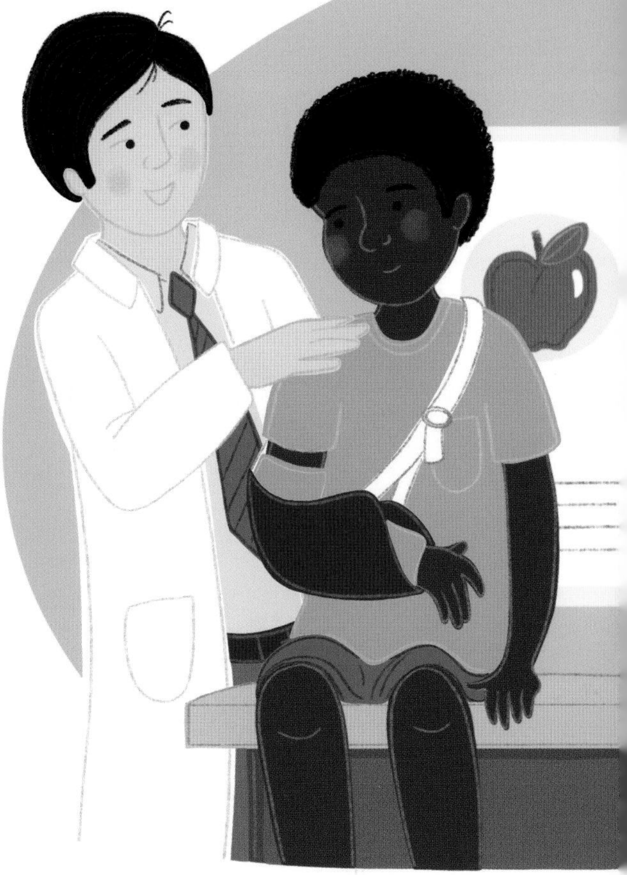

Doctor Bones puts Leo's arm in a **cast** for six weeks and gives him a **sling** to wear. The sling will help keep his arm stable.

On his way out, Leo sees Emmy. Emmy signs his new cast.

Does it hurt?

It did at first, but now not so much.

My dad is taking me to get ice cream.

Emmy's mommy is visiting radiology too.

Hello. I'm Hannah. I'll be handling your ultrasound today.

Doctor Safer has ordered an **ultrasound** for Emmy's mommy. An ultrasound uses **sound waves** to show what is going on inside a person's body.

Hannah is a diagnostic medical sonographer, or ultrasound technologist.

The ultrasound machine helps Hannah and Doctor Safer take a look inside Emmy's mommy's tummy to see how the baby is doing.

Hannah prints out a **sonogram**, or photo, for Emmy's mommy.

Can you point to the baby's nose and feet?

Emmy and her mommy are ready to head home.
But first they stop at the cafeteria before they leave.
On their way down the hall, they see Annabelle.

CAFETERIA

Annabelle has an appointment with Dr. Allbetter in the pediatric department. Dr. Allbetter is a pediatrician.

What does your pediatrician do to help you?

Annabelle's mommy fills out some paperwork at the reception desk while Annabelle sits in the waiting room. Annabelle taps her foot, nervously.

PEDIATRICS

You feeling okay, sweetie?

It's Doctor Tell. She lives next door to Annabelle. Dr. Tell is a child psychologist.

Yes, just a little nervous. I'm getting a shot today.

Don't worry. Just remember to take a deep breath. A little pinch helps keep you safe from getting sick. It'll be over before you know it.

A nurse calls Annabelle's name. It's time to see the doctor.

Annabelle is here for a **physical examination** to make sure that she is healthy.

Dr. Allbetter reviews Annabelle's vitals, weight, and height.

Okay, Annabelle, today we have to give you a shot, but I promise Nurse Lou is the best. She's going to take great care of you.

Nurse Lou comes back in with a tray. She explains the shot to Annabelle's mommy.

On her way out,
Annabelle sees Emmy again
in the cafeteria. There are lots
of doctors, nurses, and other
workers eating lunch.

FOOD SERVICE
ASSISTANT

Food service people are delivering meals to patients,
cooking, and washing dishes in the back. Together
they all keep Helping Hospital healthy and fed.

Emmy is munching apple slices
when her mommy feels a sharp pain.

Uh-oh. It looks like
Emmy's going to be a
big sister sooner than
she thought!

Daddy arrives at the hospital and heads up to help Mommy. Mimi and Grumpy sit with Emmy in the waiting room. Waiting for a baby to come can take a long time.

Lots of people from Honey Hill visit the hospital while she waits. Emmy sees . . .

Mrs. Davis standing in line at the pharmacy.

Gigi and her dad buying flowers in the gift shop.

Just then, Daddy bursts into the waiting room.

Grumpy, Mimi, and Emmy follow Daddy through the double doors. Volunteers are putting together baby hats to pass out to all the new moms.

It's finally time to meet the new baby!
Emmy curls up in the hospital bed next to her mommy.

It's been a busy day at Helping Hospital!
Everyone works very hard to keep Honey Hill
safe and healthy. Thank you, Helping Hospital!

Do you know the people who keep your town safe and healthy?

Search & Find

Around 4 million babies are born per year in the United States. How many babies did you see in Helping Hospital?

Lots of doctors work in Helping Hospital. Can you count them on each page? How many did you find?

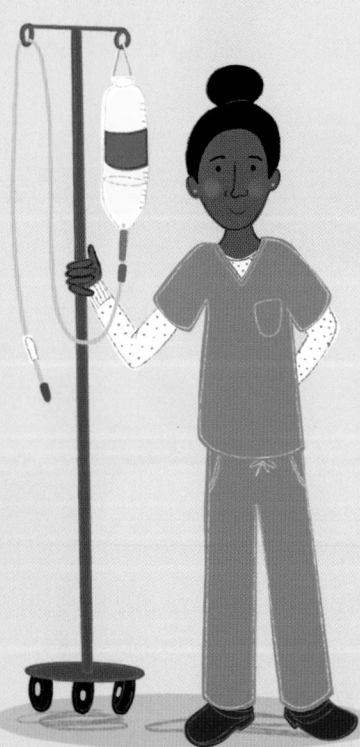

This is an IV, which stands for intravenous. Doctors and nurses use IVs to give medicine and fluids to patients to help them feel better. How many IVs can you find in Helping Hospital?

How many windows did you see on the outside of Helping Hospital?

An apple a day keeps the doctor away. Apples are rich in fiber, vitamins, minerals, and antioxidants. Can you find an apple on each page?

How many times did you find Mr. Fixit? What is he doing?

Nurses are very important to helping Helping Hospital run smoothly. How many nurses did you see?

Helping Hospital took care of a lot of people today. Can you count them all?

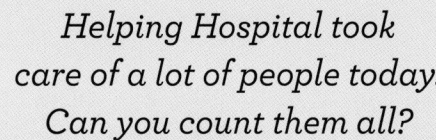

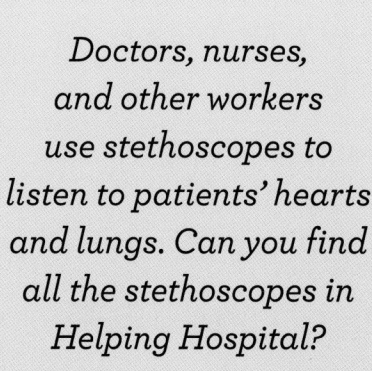

Doctors, nurses, and other workers use stethoscopes to listen to patients' hearts and lungs. Can you find all the stethoscopes in Helping Hospital?

Glossary

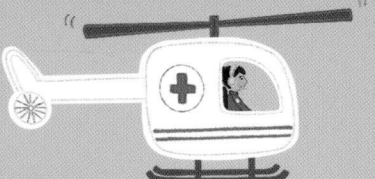

Ambulance a medically equipped vehicle that takes people to the hospital

Blood Drive an event for people to donate and collect blood to help others

Blood Pressure the pressure of blood moving through the walls of your blood vessels

Bones parts of your skeleton that protect the organs and provide support and structure for the body

Cast a covering, usually made from plaster, to protect a broken bone

Doctor someone who has medical training to help sick or injured people

Electromagnetic Radiation the movement of energy (electric and magnetic waves) through space at the speed of light

Humerus a bone in the arm that runs from the shoulder to the elbow

Medevac Helicopter used to transport someone in a medical emergency

Nurse a medically trained person who cares for other people when they are sick or hurt

Patient a person who needs and/or is receiving medical attention

Physical Examination a yearly check-up performed by a doctor to check weight, height, and vitals like blood pressure, etc.

Shot a dose of medicine given through a needle injection

Sling a loop of material used to support the weight of a broken limb

Sonogram an image produced by sound frequencies using an ultrasound machine.

Sound Waves vibrations moving through the air that we can hear and bounce off of other objects

Surgery cutting into the body to repair, remove, or adjust organs and tissues

Ultrasound a medical test that uses sound waves to create images from inside your body

Vital Signs important measurements such as temperature, pulse rate, respiration rate, and blood pressure that determine how healthy a person is

Wheelchair a chair with wheels, used by someone who can't walk

X-Ray an image created by using electromagnetic waves to photograph the inside of the body